DINO-BASKETBALL

LISA WHEELER
ILLUSTRATIONS BY BARRY GOTT

CAROLRHODA BOOKS MINNEAPOLIS

For my great-nephews:
Colin, Evan, Josiyah, Oren, Riley, and
Tyler
—L.W.

For Rose, Finn, and Nandi
—B.G.

Carolrhoda Books
A division of Lerner Publishing Group, Inc.
241 First Avenue North
Minneapolis, MN 55401 USA

For reading levels and more information,
look up this title at www.lernerbooks.com.

Library of Congress Cataloging-in-Publication Data

Wheeler, Lisa, 1963–
    Dino-basketball / by Lisa Wheeler ; illustrated by Barry Gott.
      p.   cm.
    Summary: Plant-eating dinosaurs face meat-eating dinosaurs in a
basketball game at Mastadon Square Garden.
    ISBN: 978-0-7613-6393-4 (lib. bdg. : alk. paper)
    ISBN: 978-0-7613-7149-6 (EB pdf)
    [1. Stories in rhyme. 2. Dinosaurs—Fiction. 3. Basketball—Fiction.] I.
Gott, Barry, ill. II. Title.
PZ8.3.W5668Dg 2011
[E]—dc22   2010027363

Manufactured in the United States of America
8-45161-11516-12/6/2017

Here come herds of frenzied fans.
March Madness reigns in Dino Land!

Fill the stands around the court
for Dino-Hoops—the favorite sport.

The **GRASS CLIPPERS** are the team to beat.

The underdogs are called the MEAT.

Grassy pom-poms swish and sway!

The cheerleaders are pumped today.

MEAT

POINT GUARD–T. REX
SHOOTING GUARD–RAPTOR
SMALL FORWARD–PTERODACTYL #1
POWER FORWARD–GALLIMIMUS
CENTER–ALLOSAURUS
BENCH–BARYONYX, PTERODACTYL #2,
COMPSOGNATHUS

GRASSCLIPPERS

POINT GUARD–TRICERATOPS
SHOOTING GUARD–STEGOSAURUS
SMALL FORWARD–PACHYCEPHALOSAUR
POWER FORWARD–APATOSAURUS
CENTER–DIPLODOCUS
BENCH–JOBARIA, LESOTHOSAURUS

Players take the court by storm.
Each wears a shiny uniform.

Jerseys, shorts, and sneakered feet.
Green is **Clippers**. Red is **Meat**.

It's the tip-off—center court.

Twixt the players, ref looks short.

He holds the ball. He throws it high. **Diplo** barely has to try.

A well-placed tap. It's **Clippers'** ball. Cheers resound off of every wall!

The game begins at breakneck speed.
Two points for **Stego!** **Clippers** lead.

Allo answers off the dribble.
Diplo takes it up the middle—

—**T. rex** charges from behind.
Steals the ball. It's **Meaty** time!

He drives the ball up to the hoop.
Lobs to **Raptor**—alley-oop!

Outside the baseline, **Stego** throws.
It bounces in near **Pachy's** toes.

Pachy's down the court so fast.
Scans her teammates. Needs to pass.

There's **Tricera** on the spot—
Allosaurus blocks the shot!

Then **Pterodactyl #1**
cuts in on a zigzag run.

Stego takes the charge down low!
A **Meaty** foul—two whistles blow.

Ptero #1 is through.
In comes Ptero #2.

Apatosaurus dribbles—stops—
dishes to **Triceratops.**

Triceratops is trapped—breaks loose!
He leaps. He scores! An easy deuce.

Dribble, pivot, jump, release—
two-by-two, the points increase.

Much too soon to know who wins.
Halftime's here. The show begins.

Music! Mascots! Whoops and roars!
A pyramid of dinosaurs!

Fans wave banners. Stomp their feet.
Clapping out a rockin' beat.

We will . . .
we will . . .
Chomp you!

Halftime's over. Fans are wild.
Chanting! Cheering! Teams get riled!

Compy doesn't need to stoop—
weaves through legs right toward the hoop.

A vicious slash—he's at the net.
SWISH! This game's not over yet!

Jabbing elbows. Gruesome growls.
Traveling. Tending. Flagrant fouls!

A **red** team foul can only mean
it's a free throw for the **green**.

Behind the foul line, **Pachy** aims.
Two shots. Two points. Back to the game.

The **Clipper** team is in control.
Leso takes it to the hole.

The little guy goes for the dunk.
Hits the rim. His hopes are sunk.

KLUNK!!

The **Clipper's** coach demands a win.
Leso's out. **Jobaria's** in.

Back and forth. Forth and back.
Trusty scoreboard—keeping track.

M 51   08:40   G 50

#66 JOBARIA

On the sidelines, coaches pace,
determined scowls upon each face.

Dino-TV camera pans,
zooms in on some famous fans.

Though they wear a lame disguise,
everybody knows these guys.

Stego takes a shot—denied!
The ball is back on the **red** team's side.

Pivots left, then fakes right,
Raptor sees no **Meat** in sight.

"Pass it!" Gallimimus cries.
She's blocked by Diplo's massive size.

So Raptor takes an outside shot.
En fuego! Ouch! The Meat is hot!

Then **Jobar** takes it to the hole.
Fans are breathless—lose control!

Clock is ticking. **Score** is tied.
But **Meat** has talent on its side.

T. rex passes. **Galli** fakes.
Shoots the ball with no mistakes.

She made the shot! The points are sweet!
Red team wins! Our champs!—the **Meat!**

Sneakers squeak on wooden floors.
The court is stormed by dinosaurs.

holds the trophy high.
The   fans cheer. The coaches cry.

They celebrate—cut down the net.

This was their finest season yet.

The end is here, but you can bet . . .

Tickets go on sale at noon—
Dino-Football's coming soon!